# More Stories for ...

*In the same series:*

The Collins Book of Stories for Four-Year-Olds
The Collins Book of Stories for Five-Year-Olds
The Collins Book of Stories for Six-Year-Olds
The Collins Book of Stories for Seven-Year-Olds
The Collins Book of Stories for Eight-Year-Olds
More Stories for Six-Year-Olds

# More Stories for Five-Year-Olds

Collected by Julia Eccleshare

*Illustrated by Dave McTaggart*

Collins

An *imprint of* HarperCollins*Publishers*

First published in Great Britain in Young Lions 1994

3  5  7  9  10  9  6  4  2

Young Lions is an imprint of Collins Childrens Books,
part of HarperCollins Publishers Ltd,
77/85 Fulham Palace Road,
Hammersmith,
London W6 8JB

ISBN 0 00 674722–1

Set in Ehrhardt
Printed and bound in Great Britain by
HarperCollins Manufacturing, Glasgow

# Contents

The Flood   7
*Ruth Ainsworth*

Simple Jack   23
*retold by James Reeves*

Helping Lizzie Sleep   34
*Adèle Geras*

Mashenka and the Bear   44
*James Riordan*

Pyjama Dance   52
*Sophie Hannah*

I Don't Like This House!   69
*Irene Yates*

The Star Money   76
*Anne Rockwell*

The Wonderful Washing Machine   80
*Linda Allen*

The King with Dirty Feet   89
*Pomme Clayton*

# CONTENTS

The Brave Cat and the Little Girl          99
   *Margaret Mayo*

The Story of the Thick Fat Pancake         108
   *Traditional*

Jasper the Vain Toucan                     116
   *Angela McAllister*

The Toffee Join                            125
   *William Mayne*

Acknowledgements                          151

# The Flood

## Ruth Ainsworth

The shed was near the house. It was dark because it had only one small window, and that was covered with cobwebs. There were some tools in the shed, a spade and a rake and a hoe, and a pile of old sacks. There was something else as well, that not many people knew about. If you stood quite still in the shed, without moving a hand or a foot, you could hear the crackle of straw and perhaps a tiny cry.

The crackle of straw and the cry came from a box standing in a corner. In the box were a mother cat and her three newborn kittens. The cat's name was Minnie and her kittens were named One, Two, and Three. When they were big and could wash themselves and drink milk from a saucer, they would go to homes of their own. Then someone would give them proper names. But One, Two, and Three did very well to start with.

Sometimes a dog barked.

"What is that?" asked One, his little legs shaking.

"It is only Prince, the dog," purred Minnie. "He is taking care of us. He barks when he sees a stranger coming."

Sometimes a door banged.

"What is that?" mewed Two, shuddering like a jelly.

"It is only the wind blowing the door

8

shut," purred Minnie. "Now the wind won't get into our snug bed."

Sometimes the coalman tipped the coal out with a sound like thunder.

"What is that?" cried Three, hiding her face in her mother's fur.

"It is only the coalman," purred Minnie. "His coal will make the kitchen fire blaze and burn. I will take you into the kitchen for a treat, when you are bigger, if you are very good."

A lady named Mrs Plum lived in the kitchen. She wore a white apron. Every day she brought Minnie's meal to her, in a blue dish. When Minnie had finished her food, the dish was as clean as if it had been washed.

One night, when the kittens were fast asleep, curled like furry balls beside their mother, a storm blew up. The door and window of the shed rattled. The rain fell in floods on the roof. There were terrible claps of thunder and bright, zigzag flashes of lightning. Even Minnie felt frightened. The river ran at the bottom of the garden, on the other side of the garden wall, and she could hear it roaring by. It sounded like a fierce, growling animal.

"What is wrong? What has happened?" mewed One, Two, and Three.

"I don't know, my dears," said Minnie. "But we must go to sleep and not be frightened."

But Minnie herself was very frightened and so were the three kittens. No one could get to sleep while the storm was raging.

The kittens were so young that their eyes were not yet open. But Minnie's eyes shone like green lamps. She could see, under the door of the shed, a trickle of water. The trickle grew into a puddle. The puddle grew into a wave. The wave came nearer and nearer across the floor. Then it reached the box in the corner.

Minnie did not like water. She did not

even like getting her paws wet on the wet grass. She was very, very frightened to see the water creeping under the door and spreading across the whole floor.

"If it gets any deeper," she thought to herself, "I shall take the kittens in my mouth, one at a time, and jump on to the wheelbarrow, and then up on to the shelf where the flowerpots are stacked. I don't think the water could get as high as that."

The water flowed faster and faster under the door until it was inches deep. Just when Minnie was getting ready to take a kitten in her mouth and spring on to the wheelbarrow, and then on to the shelf, a strange thing happened. The wooden box began to move about. It was floating. It was floating like a boat.

There was a thick layer of straw in the bottom of the box and an old woollen jersey. The kittens stayed dry and warm while they floated on their bed. They did not mind at all because they could not see the water as their eyes were shut.

Suddenly there was a clap of thunder and a great blast of wind. The door of the shed blew open with a bang. The water rushed in and the box swirled round and round. Then it floated out of the shed into the garden.

The river had risen so high that it swept over the garden wall. The box swished over the wall and sailed along the river which was now wide and deep like a sea. It was too dark to see exactly where they were going. Minnie cuddled her babies close to her while the rain fell in torrents. The kittens were soon fast asleep, and though Minnie was sure she would never get a wink herself, she dozed off as well.

When the morning came, they were in a watery world. There was water in front of them. Water behind. Water all round. Minnie had not known there could be so much water in one place. Strange things floated by. Branches of trees which had been torn off by the storm. Tables and chairs and pillows and cushions that had been washed out of houses. Sacks and straw and even a dog kennel. Minnie was pleased to see that the kennel was empty.

Nothing stopped Minnie from bringing up her kittens as well as she could, so she washed them just as carefully as if they had been on dry land. When she had finished One's face, he mewed in an excited voice:

"I can see! I can see! I can see you and Two and Three and the water and everything!"

He frisked about with joy and Minnie was afraid he might fall out of the box.

Before long, Two and Three could see as well and they spent most of the day calling out:

"What's that? What's that? What's that?" or else: "Why is the water shiny? Why is it brown?" and many other questions, some of which Minnie could not answer.

Though the kittens were well and happy, Minnie was worried. The kittens were fat as butter and could drink her warm milk whenever they wished. But there was nothing for *her* to eat, no milk – no fish – no liver. Nothing at all.

The other thing that worried her was that she could not bring her children up properly in a box floating on the water. How would they learn to lap milk from a saucer? Or walk upstairs? Or climb trees? Or catch mice? Minnie had brought up so many families of kittens that she knew exactly how the job ought to be done.

Now that the rain had stopped the floods began to go down. The river was no longer wild and roaring. Hedges and bushes could be seen that had been under the water a few hours before. When the box drifted near the bank and was caught on the branches of a willow tree, Minnie

14

knew what she must do.

Quick as a flash, she snatched up the nearest kitten, who happened to be Two, and climbed up the tree with him. She dashed back for One and Three and the little family were soon perched on the damp, slippery branch of a willow, instead of cuddled in a floating cradle filled with straw.

"This is a horrid place!" mewed One.

"I shall fall into the water and be drowned!" mewed Two.

"How are we to sleep without a bed?" mewed Three.

Minnie was not comfortable herself as she was trying to look after three young kittens as well as hold on, but she did not approve of grumbling.

"The river is going down," she said cheerfully. "Tomorrow or the next day I shall carry you home, one at a time, in my mouth. Till then, you must be good kittens and do what I tell you."

"Do you know the way home?" asked One. "We must have floated a long way in our wooden box."

Minnie was not certain that she *did* know the way, but she replied firmly:

"Of course I know the way. The river brought us here. I shall just follow the river and it will lead us home. Anyhow, all sensible cats know the way home. They never get lost."

All day and all night Minnie took care of her kittens. She fed them and washed them and sang to them, and when they slept she kept them from falling off the branch. When they were awake and wanted to play, she told them stories. She told them about the red kitchen fire that ate black coal. She told them about mice with long tails who lived in holes and were fun to chase. She told them about dear Mrs Plum and her white apron and her warm, comfortable lap.

When the *next* morning came, the river

had gone right down. The ground was wet and muddy, but it was not under water. They could see the path running along the river bank.

"I shall take one of you home now," said Minnie.

"Take me!" "No, me!" "No, ME!" mewed the three kittens.

"I shall take Three first because she is the smallest," said Minnie. "Now, One and Two, be brave and sensible and hold on tightly."

"What will happen if we fall off?" asked One and Two.

"You would lose one of your nine lives," said Minnie. "Then you would have only eight left."

She took little Three in her mouth, climbed down the tree to the ground, and ran off along the river bank. She felt sure she was going the right way and that every step was bringing her nearer home. The wet mud was cold and nasty to her feet, but she did not mind. If only her three kittens were safe in front of the kitchen fire, she would never mind anything again!

Little Three squirmed and squiggled and seemed to get heavier and heavier. When at last Minnie padded slowly through the gate and up the path to the back door, she could hardly drag one foot after the other.

"Miaow! Miaow!" she cried as loudly as she could. "Miaow!"

In a second the door opened and there stood dear Mrs Plum in her white apron.

"Oh, Minnie! Minnie!" she cried, gathering Minnie and Three up in her arms, and not minding at all about the mud they left on her apron. "I thought I should never see you again!"

At first Minnie purred loudly and smiled, but she knew the job was not yet finished. She began to kick and struggle till Mrs Plum put her down on the floor.

Then she ran to the back door and mewed for it to be opened.

"I know," said Mrs Plum. "I understand. You must go back for the others. Wait a moment and I will come too, I'll just make Three safe and comfortable. I kept a bed ready for you all."

There, on the hearth-rug, was another box with a soft blanket inside. Mrs Plum cuddled Three into the blanket, and Three sat and stared at the fire with round blue eyes. So *this* was the monster who ate black coal!

Mrs Plum put on her coat and hat and took a basket with a lid and opened the door. Minnie ran ahead so quickly that Mrs Plum could only just keep up. They were both tired when they got to the willow tree. Mrs Plum stood at the bottom while Minnie climbed up and found her two kittens cold and shivering, but quite safe.

"We've kept all our nine lives, Mother!" they called out.

"That's my good kittens!" said Minnie, carrying them down to the ground, where Mrs Plum stroked them and petted them and tucked them into the basket, which was lined with flannel. There was just room for Minnie as well. Then Mrs Plum carried the heavy basket home. She had to change hands when one arm ached.

When they were back in the warm kitchen, Mrs Plum gave Minnie a good meal. She had sardines and a dish of corn-flakes and three saucers of milk. Then they all five settled down for a cosy afternoon by the fire. Mrs Plum knitted in her rocking chair, and the three kittens watched the red fire eating coal and stared at the brass rim of the fender and the plates on the dresser and all the other wonderful things.

They kept looking at Mrs Plum's ball of wool.

"I don't know why, but I should like to roll that ball of wool all over the floor," said One.

"So should I!" said Two and Three.

"That would be very naughty of you indeed," said Minnie. "But I wanted to do just the same when I was a kitten."

"And did you do it?" asked the three kittens.

"Yes, I'm afraid I did!" said Minnie.

She purred and smiled and dozed, as the clock ticked on the wall and the fire crackled and Mrs Plum clicked her knitting needles.

# Simple Jack

## retold by James Reeves

Jack lived with his mother in a cottage beside a common. He was the laziest boy in the world. His mother earned a living for them both by spinning, and when she wasn't spinning she was washing or mending, and when she wasn't washing or mending she was getting a meal ready. But all Jack would do was to sit under the apple tree in summer sucking grasses, and in the chimney corner in winter keeping his toes warm.

At last his mother could put up with it no longer.

"Out you go," said she one fine Monday morning. "Out you go, and earn yourself a living or you shan't stay here any more. You're old enough to get work for yourself now, so don't come back till you've made some money to help pay for the food you eat!"

Slowly Jack got up from his seat by the fire and went out. He hired himself to a farmer, and by the end of the day he had earned sixpence. Holding it in his hand, he started for home; but, crossing over a brook, he slipped on a wet stone and dropped the sixpence. It was nowhere to be found. There was nothing for it but to go home and tell his mother what had happened.

"Why, you stupid boy!" said his mother. "I could have done with sixpence, but now you've lost it. You should have put it in your pocket. Then you'd have kept it safe and sound. See you if you can do better tomorrow."

Well, on Tuesday morning Jack went off once more, though he would rather have sat by the fire all day. This time he hired himself to a dairyman, and at the end of the day he was given a pail of milk for wages. So remembering what his mother had said, he emptied the pail into the pocket of his coat and began to jog along home. Of course the milk was all wasted, and his clothes were soaked into the bargain.

"Why, you silly, good-for-nothing scamp!" cried his mother, when he told her what had happened. "We could have done with some nice new milk for supper, but now there's none – thanks to your foolishness. You should have carried the pail on your head, then you would have brought it home safe and sound."

On Wednesday morning Jack went off again to work for the farmer, and for his day's work the farmer gave him a fine pat of butter.

"Now what did she tell me to do with it?" thought Jack. Then he remembered. He clapped the butter on top of his head and started for home. But it was a warm evening, and soon the butter got stuck in his hair and ran down behind his ears, and some of it fell to the ground, and all of it was spoilt.

Jack's mother was angrier than ever.

"It's too bad!" she said. "I could have done with some good dairy butter if you hadn't gone and spoilt it all. What a donkey you are! Whatever did you put it on your head for? You should have carried it in your hand."

Well, on Thursday morning Jack set off once more, trudging away across the common to see a baker in the village; and all day he worked for the baker, and the baker gave him nothing but a black cat for his day's work. He had too many cats in the bakery and was glad to get rid of one.

When he got home, he had nothing at all to show for his day's work except a pair of hands covered all over with bites and scratches.

"What did you get today?" asked Jack's mother.

"Why, the baker gave me a black cat, mother," said Jack, "and I carried her in my hands like you told me yesterday, and she scratched me till I had to let her go."

"Deary me, deary me!" said his mother. "Aren't you the stupidest ninny ever born? You shouldn't have tried to carry a cat home in your hands. You should have tied a string round her neck and pulled her along after you. It's very vexing," she went on. "We could have done with a good cat to keep the mice from the larder!"

On Friday morning Jack went off to the butcher's shop and hired himself to the butcher for the day. Now the butcher was a kind man and knew that Jack's mother was poor, so at the end of the day he gave Jack a leg of good lean mutton. Jack thanked the butcher and left the shop. He thought very carefully about what his mother had told him the day before, and this time he was determined to make no mistake. So he took a piece of string from his pocket and pulled the meat along behind him in the road.

When she saw the meat, all dirty and spoilt, Jack's mother was more annoyed than ever.

"Oh, you dunderhead!" she cried. "When *will* you learn sense? We could have done with a fine lean leg of mutton for dinner tomorrow and you've as good as thrown it away! Fancy bringing it home like that!"

"But what *should* I have done, mother?" Jack asked.

"If you'd had two penn'orth of common

sense, you'd have lifted it on your shoulder and carried it home like that. Be off to bed with you, for there's not a bite of supper in the house. The way you're going on, we shall both starve, and that's the truth!"

Well, next morning was Saturday, and once more Jack set out to see what he could earn. He hired himself to a cowman that he knew, and at the end of the day the cowman gave him a donkey. So remembering once more what his mother had told him, Jack hoisted the donkey on to his shoulders, and staggered off home. The animal gave poor Jack a great deal of trouble, for it did not like being carried upside down on his shoulders. However, Jack was determined to get home safely *this* time, and not lose his day's wages. So he grasped the donkey's legs with all his strength and took no notice of its braying and kicking.

Now it so happened that in a great

house beside the highroad lived a rich man, and he had one beautiful daughter who was both deaf and dumb. She had never heard nor spoken a word in all her life. But the doctor had told her father that, if the girl could be made to laugh, she might be cured. And the rich man had spent years and years trying to make his beautiful daughter laugh, but the harder he tried the sadder she looked, till everyone gave up hope of ever having her cured.

As Jack was passing the house with the donkey upside down on his back, it happened that the girl was looking out of an upstairs window. Never had she seen such a thing in all her life! There must surely be nothing funnier in the world than to see a great country lad staggering along the road with a donkey kicking and braying upside down on his back: at first the girl could not believe her eyes, and then she began to smile, and then

her smile grew broader and broader until she laughed out loud; she laughed so loud and long that the tears came to her eyes, and scarcely knowing what she was doing, she called out to everyone in the house:

"Oh, c-come and look! J-just come and look! Did you ever see such a thing? It's the funniest thing you ever saw!"

Well, the girl's father and all their friends were delighted that at last the girl had spoken, and they were so pleased that they ran out into the road and called Jack inside. So in he went, donkey and all, and the girl was so pleased with him that she wouldn't let him go.

Nothing would please the rich man's daughter but that she should marry Jack and have him to live with for always. And very happy they were in a great house that the rich man bought for them. They kept the donkey in a field at the back of the house, and Jack's mother came to live with them for the rest of her life. Jack became a fine gentleman and had servants to wait on him and see that he never did any more work from that time on.

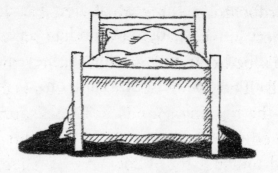

# Helping Lizzie Sleep

## Adèle Geras

There were five people in the Meadowes family, and six if you counted Mimi the cat. They were all wonderful sleepers except for Lizzie, the youngest child, who was *four* years old. Mimi was the best sleeper of them all, curling up into a tight ball of tabby fur on any comfortable chair she could find. She was also fond of small spaces, and especially enjoyed a snooze in a cardboard box, the ironing basket, or a corner of the cupboard in Mum and Dad's bedroom. This didn't worry them at all. They were also excellent sleepers and the buzzing sounds of Dad's snoring echoed round the house the moment his head touched the pillow. It was a family joke now, but when Lizzie was very small, she was frightened by the noise, and thought that there had to be a dragon in bed with her parents.

Lizzie was the only person who heard the snores, because both her brother Mick and her sister Suzanne went straight off to sleep immediately, leaving her alone and awake and feeling sorry for herself.

"We must do something to help Lizzie get to sleep at night," said Mum at breakfast one day. "She looks so tired . . . too tired to go to the nursery."

"But I want to go to the nursery," said Lizzie, pouting into her cornflakes. "And I want to sleep too, but the more I think about it, the harder it is."

"I think," said Mick "that we should have a competition to see who can tell the magic story that will help Lizzie get to sleep."

"But if I'm listening to a story, I'll be staying awake," Lizzie said. "If it's an interesting story."

"Perhaps," said Dad "we should have a competition for the most boring story . . . the one that puts you to sleep fastest. I'll go first. I bet I could tell the most boring story in the world."

So that night, Dad had his turn. His story was very boring indeed. It was all about a farmer who had thousands of sheep he wanted to move from one field to another. They all had to jump over a fence and the farmer counted them as they jumped over. This story was working quite well, until Dad made a dreadful mistake and said that one little sheep was too small to get over the fence. Lizzie was wide awake at once, and wanted to know all about this sheep. Why was it so small? Was it ill? Where was its mother? Did it have brothers and sisters? Maybe there was Something Bad in the second field that no one but the little sheep knew about? By the time Dad had answered all Lizzie's questions, she was a little happier about the sheep but no nearer being sleepy. He, on the other hand, looked as though he was just about ready to turn into a snoring dragon right there on the end of her bed.

"Your story wasn't a great success," said Mum the next morning. "I think lullabies are the best. I shall sing Lizzie some of my magic lullabies tonight and you'll see, that'll do the trick."

Mum's lullabies were magic, but not quite in the way she intended. They turned out to be the only thing in the world that could wake up Mimi the cat and make her leave the room.

"Oh dear," said Mum. "I suppose I'm not a very good singer. Even Mimi gets up and leaves when I open my mouth."

The next night it was Suzanne's turn. She was already at school.

"I know," she said. "I'll tell you all about my geography homework. That's enough to put anyone to sleep."

But Lizzie loved the geography. "Tell me more about rivers," she said. "Where they come from and where they go to and also tell me about all that ice slicing through the mountains. I like that bit. And have you learned about dinosaurs yet? Will you tell me when you do?"

Poor Suzanne sighed. "The trouble with you is," she said, "nothing at all bores you. You're interested in everything. That's probably why you can't sleep. Sleep is a bit dull, unless you have nice dreams every night."

The next day Mick said: "Lizzie will sleep well tonight. I know she will."

"How do you know?" asked Lizzie.

"Wait and see," said Mick, buttering another slice of toast.

That night Mick sat on Lizzie's bed.

"Do you know what this is?" he asked her, pointing to her duvet.

"It's my duvet," said Lizzie. "Silly!"

"It's not only a duvet," said Mick. "It's a special magic country, called the Land of Eiderdown. And the people who live there are in terrible trouble."

"Why? I can't see any people anyway."

"Can't you?" Mick said. "Look down there . . . can't you see slopes of hills and little houses, with trees shading them? Can't you see tiny people walking about in the gardens?"

Lizzie looked. The golden light shining in from the landing fell on her duvet in such a way as to make shadows in which she could see . . . she thought she could see . . . yes, she really could see everything that Mick was describing.

"Yes," she said. "I can see everything. But why is everyone so unhappy?"

"Because they can't sleep. There's a giant who lives deep, deep in the earth under their country and every night when they want to sleep this giant tosses and turns and gets into and out of her bed and makes all the house in the Land of Eiderdown go up and down like roller coasters. This giant makes terrible earthquakes and landslides . . ."

"Who's the giant?" Lizzie asked.

"Can't you guess?"

"Is it me?"

Mick nodded. Lizzie nearly started crying.

"What shall I do? I don't want anyone not to sleep. I don't want to make the whole land move about like that. What shall I do?"

"It's easy . . ." said Mick. "First of all you lie quite still."

"Like this?"

"Yes, that's lovely. Now close your eyes, and we'll do a register of all the people in Eiderdown. You can do it in your head. Just think of all the names you possibly can, in your head, and then say them over to me, and I'll tell you when they're properly asleep . . ."

"Milly . . . Sally . . . Molly . . . Polly . . . Dolly . . . Holly . . . Mimi . . . Jenny . . ."

One by one, Lizzie said out loud all the names she could think of. She went through the names of her dolls, her friends and everyone from stories that she could remember, including the Old Woman who lived in the shoe and her twelve children. As she said each name, Mick whispered the magic word "Sleeping" and then all the "Sleepings" slid into one another like wind shushing through the branches of trees, and Lizzie's eyelids grew heavier and heavier and drooped and then closed tight.

In the morning, Mick said: "I did it. I

made Lizzie sleep, and I bet she sleeps tonight as well."

"Oh, I will," said Lizzie. "I don't want to disturb . . ."

"Sh," said Mick. "Don't tell them. It's a secret."

Lizzie never told her secret, but every night she lay under her duvet and imagined the people of the Land of Eiderdown sleeping quietly in their beds, no longer afraid of the Lizzie giant who used to make earthquakes and landslides in the place where they lived.

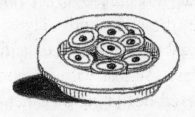

# Mashenka
# and the Bear
## James Riordan

An old peasant and his wife had a grand-daughter, Mashenka. One summer's day, the little girl's friends called on her to go mushrooming with them in the meadow.

"Granny, Grandad," cried Mashenka. "May I go out to play? I'll bring you lots of mushrooms, I promise."

"Run along then," the old pair said, "but mind you don't go near the forest or else the wolves or bears will get you."

Off skipped the girls towards the meadow at the forest edge. Mashenka knew that the best and biggest mushrooms grew beneath the trees and bushes in the forest. Almost without noticing it, she wandered out of sight of her friends. She moved from tree to tree, from bush to bush, picking a basketful of mushrooms – reds and yellows, browns and whites. All the while she went deeper and deeper into the forest. Suddenly, she looked up and realized she was lost.

"Hell-oooo! Hell-oooo!" she called.

There was no reply.

Someone heard her nonetheless.

From the trees came a rustling and a cracking, and out stepped a big brown bear. When he set eyes on the little girl, he threw up his arms in joy.

"Aha!" he cried. "You'll make a fine servant for me, my pretty one."

Taking the girl roughly by the arm, he

dragged her to his cottage in the depths of the dark wood. Once inside, he growled at her, "Now stoke the fire, cook some porridge and make my home clean and tidy."

There now began a miserable life in the bear's cottage for poor Mashenka. Day after day she toiled from dawn to dusk, afraid the bear would eat her. All the while she thought of how she could escape. Finally, an idea came to her.

"Mister Bear," she said politely, "may I go home for a day to show my grandparents I am alive and well?"

"Certainly not," growled the bear. "You'll never leave here. If you have a message I'll take it myself."

That was just what Mashenka had planned. She baked some cherry pies, piled them on a dish and fetched a big basket. Then she called the bear.

"Mister Bear, I'll put the pies in this basket for you to carry home. Remember, though, not to open the basket and don't touch the pies. I'll be watching. When you set off I'll climb on to the roof to keep an eye on you."

"All right, pretty one," grumbled the bear. "Just let me take a nap before I go."

No sooner was the bear asleep than Mashenka quickly climbed on to the roof and made a lifelike figure out of a pole, her coat and headscarf. Then she scrambled down, squeezed into the basket and pulled the dish of cherry pies over her head. When the bear woke up and saw the basket ready, he hoisted it on to his broad back and set off for the village.

Through the trees he ambled with his load and soon he felt tired and footsore. Stopping by a tree stump, he sank down to rest, thinking of eating a cherry pie. But just as he was about to open the basket, he heard Mashenka's voice.

"Don't sit there all day and don't you touch those pies."

Glancing round he could just see her figure on his roof.

"My, my, that maid has sharp eyes," he mumbled to himself. Up he got and continued on his way.

On and on he went, carrying the heavy load. Soon he came upon another tree stump.

"I'll just take a rest and eat a cherry pie," he thought, puffing and panting. Yet once again Mashenka's muffled voice was heard.

"Don't sit down and don't touch those pies. Go straight to the village as I told you."

He looked back but could no longer see his house.

"Well, I'll be jiggered!" he exclaimed. "She's got eyes like a hawk, that girl."

So on he went.

Through the trees he shuffled, down

into the valley, on through groves of ash, up grassy knolls until, finally, he emerged into a meadow.

"I must rest my poor feet," he sighed. "And I'll just have one small pie to refresh me. She surely cannot see me now."

But from out of nowhere came a distant voice.

"I can see you! I can see you! Don't you touch those cherry pies! Go on, Mister Bear."

The bear was puzzled, even scared.

"What an extraordinary girl she is," he growled, hurrying across the field.

At last he arrived at the village, stopped at Mashenka's door and knocked loudly.

"Open up, open up!" he cried gruffly. "I've brought a present from your granddaughter."

The moment they heard his voice, however, dogs came running from all the yards. Their barking startled him so much, he left the basket at the door and made off towards the forest without a backward glance.

How surprised Mashenka's grandparents were when they opened the door, found the basket and saw no one in sight.

Grandad lifted up the lid, stared hard and could scarcely believe his eyes. For there beneath the cherry pies sat the little girl, alive and well.

Granny and Grandad both danced with joy, hugged Mashenka and said what a clever girl she was to trick the bear. Soon all her friends heard the news and came running to hug and kiss her too. Mashenka was so happy.

In the meantime, deep in the forest, the old bear had reached home and shouted to the figure on the roof to make his tea. Of course, it did not take him long to learn that the wise young girl had tricked him.

# Pyjama Dance

## Sophie Hannah

Lisa sat bolt upright in bed, her arms firmly folded. She had no intention of lying down, let alone going to sleep. Mum came in to say goodnight, but Lisa stuck her nose in the air and pretended not to hear her.

"I see," said Mum, sitting down on the edge of Lisa's bed. "You're in a sulk."

"I am *not* in a sulk," Lisa corrected her.

"I'm on strike. There's a difference between sulking and being on strike."

"Ah." Mum suppressed a smile. "What sort of strike?"

"A sleeping strike," Lisa told her. "I refuse to sleep in these horrible pyjamas any more. You've been promising to buy me some new ones for ages and you still haven't. So I've decided I'm never, ever going to sleep again until you do!"

Mum laughed. "Suit yourself," she said, "but don't blame me if you get very tired."

Lisa was close to tears. "You don't understand," she told Mum. "How would you like to sleep in these old things?" She jumped out of bed and paraded her pyjamas up and down the room to prove her point.

They were baggy, and worn thin at the knees and elbows. Their colour, once white, was now that light grey that all white clothes seem to become over time. Lisa had worn them for as long as she could remember. They must be as old as me, she thought.

"Well?" She waited for Mum's answer.

"Well," said Mum, "I agree you need new pyjamas. I couldn't afford them before, but now that I've got a new job, I can." Lisa's frown turned into a big smile.

"But," Mum added quickly, before Lisa could get too excited, "you'll have to wait. I might not be able to go shopping until next Friday."

"Friday!" Lisa groaned. "That means a whole week more in these horrid pyjamas! What if a handsome prince comes to visit me in the night?"

"He'll fall in love with you on the spot and not care two hoots about your pyjamas," Mum reassured her. "Will you go to sleep now?"

"No," said Lisa stubbornly. "I'm still on strike."

"Fine," Mum grinned. "See if I care."

Lisa scowled after her as she left the

room. She knew Mum didn't take her seriously, and she was determined to prove that she meant business. I must stay awake, she told herself firmly. Mum had turned the light off on her way downstairs and Lisa didn't dare turn it back on again, which meant that reading was impossible. Lisa wondered what she could possibly do all night. The thought of nine hours just sitting up in bed made her yawn.

Eventually Lisa decided to look out of her bedroom window because she couldn't think of anything else to do. She drew her curtains wide open. It was very dark. At first she could hardly see her own back garden, but then the blurred forms of trees became clearer and Lisa could see her clothes and Mum's dangling from the washing line. On the other side of the fence there was another garden, much neater and tidier than Lisa's, belonging to a house on the next street.

Lisa wondered who lived there. A light

was on in the back bedroom that faced hers exactly, and Lisa could make out definite shapes behind the curtain: a cupboard, a chair, a bed right next to the window, just like hers was.

Suddenly a person seemed to appear in the room, a person of about Lisa's height. Probably a girl the same age as me, Lisa thought to herself. She watched carefully as the small shadow bent over, and after a moment or two she heard music playing. It seemed to drift lightly across both gardens and into Lisa's room, the soft notes just reaching her ear.

Lisa couldn't help feeling a twinge of jealousy. It seemed unfair that the shadow-girl should have a record player in her bedroom, all to herself, *and* be allowed to stay up so late, long after Lisa's own bedtime.

To her surprise, the shadow began to dance in time with the music. Lisa moved closer to the window and stared in amazement. She had never seen dancing like

56

this before in her whole life.

First the shadow pirouetted across the room, then it spun several full circles, balancing only on one leg, while the other moved horizontally through the air, faster and faster with every turn. Lisa could hardly believe that someone of her age, or about her age, was such a graceful and brilliant dancer.

As the music slowed down and the notes became deeper and longer, the shadow drifted elegantly from quick, twirling movements to slow, deliberate ones. To Lisa, the shadow's arms looked like long tree branches swaying delicately in the wind. As she watched, Lisa forgot what time it was and how long the shadow-girl had been dancing. It was so beautiful that she would have been happy to watch for ever.

Eventually, though, the music and the dancing stopped, much to Lisa's disappointment, and the light went out. Lisa felt far too excited to sleep. She simply had to find out who the shadow-girl was. Anyone who danced so well was definitely worth making friends with. It occurred to Lisa that the shadow-girl might not want to be friends with someone who wore such tatty pyjamas, and who was about as graceful as a one-legged elephant.

Lisa vowed to herself that she would learn to dance, and then, with her new pyjamas which Mum would soon buy her, she would be the perfect best friend for the shadow-girl. As these comforting thoughts floated through her mind, Lisa's eyes began to close and she finally fell asleep, totally forgetting that she was supposed to be on a stay-awake strike.

"How's the strike going?" Mum asked her at breakfast the next morning.

"Very well," said Lisa. "I didn't sleep one wink." She could tell Mum didn't believe her, but she didn't care about that any more, now that she had something much more important to think about. "Mum, who lives in the house across the back from us?" Lisa tried not to sound too eager.

Mum thought for a minute. "Mr and Mrs . . . oh, what's their name? Hold on, I'll think of it in a minute." Lisa held her breath.

"Thomas!" Mum exclaimed. "Mr and Mrs Thomas."

"Haven't they got any children?" Lisa asked, knowing that they must have.

"Yes. Now, let me think," Mum muttered. "My memory's hopeless."

"A girl?" Lisa suggested helpfully. "About my age?"

"Yes, that's right," Mum nodded. "I think her name's Zoe. In fact, I'm sure it's Zoe. She's a bit younger than you. Why are you so interested in the Thomases all of a sudden, anyway?"

Lisa smiled to herself but didn't answer. There was one more thing she had to ask Mum, and she asked it. "Can I have ballet lessons?"

Mum laughed. "Ballet lessons? You really are in a strange mood this morning!"

"I know someone who has ballet lessons," Lisa said, not sure whether this was strictly true, since she had never actually spoken to Zoe Thomas. "She says it's really good fun."

"Then get her to teach you," Mum suggested. "That's what friends are for."

Lisa didn't answer. Mum had given her a brilliant idea. What better way to make friends with Zoe than by asking her for dancing lessons? Lisa could even pay her a little bit out of her pocket money. Zoe would surely be flattered, and they would end up being best friends and dancing partners. Lisa might even learn to dance as well as Zoe.

"I'm going out," Lisa told Mum, jumping off her chair so quickly that she almost knocked it over. "I'm going to call for Zoe Thomas."

"That's a good idea, love," said Mum, but Lisa was already running out of the door and down the drive. "Zoe's got a brother too!" Mum called after her. "His name is Gareth!" But Lisa wasn't paying attention. She wasn't interested in Zoe's brother.

Once Lisa had found the right house, she rang the doorbell and stood nervously in the porch. She hoped someone would let her in quickly because there was a group of boys playing football in the road, and they looked like the sort of boys who would aim the ball at her head just for fun.

One of them noticed her suddenly and said to his friends, "There's a girl." The football playing stopped, and all the boys seemed to examine Lisa carefully, as if they had never seen a girl before.

Lisa rang the bell again and prayed for somebody to open the door. The boys looked grubby and rude, and she wanted to get away from them as soon as possible. But, to her horror, she noticed that one of them was walking right up to her, carrying the big, orange football under his arm. Lisa thought he might drop it right on her head. She took two steps backwards.

"What are you scared of?" the boy asked her. He was slightly taller than she was, with sandy blond hair and lots of freckles.

"I'm not scared," Lisa said angrily. "And I'm especially not scared of you!"

"Good," said the boy, "because that's my doorbell you're ringing. That's my house."

The other boys began to giggle in the

road. "Gareth's in love!" they chanted. "Gareth's got a girlfriend!"

Gareth, who Lisa now knew to be Zoe's brother, turned round and shouted, "Shut up, idiots!" He turned back to Lisa. "What do you want?" he asked.

"I want to see Zoe," Lisa told him. "Is she in?"

"She's in, but she can't come to the door," said Gareth. "She's sprained her ankle and she has to stay in bed."

Lisa was puzzled. The shadow-dancer certainly hadn't had a sprained ankle. "Did she sprain it this morning?" Lisa asked.

"No, two days ago," said Gareth, "and she hasn't been able to walk since then."

"But . . . I saw her dancing last night," Lisa was confused. "She was brilliant. I wanted her to teach me. How can she dance like that if she can't even walk?"

Gareth had gone very red in the face. He kept looking over his shoulder at his friends. "How should I know?" he grunted. "She'll be okay in a couple of days, anyway. Why don't you come back then?" He went back to his friends and they began to play football again.

Lisa walked home, bewildered. She wondered if Gareth were lying, but why on earth would he want to stop her from seeing Zoe?

When she got home, there was a big parcel on the kitchen table. "It's for you," Mum told her. "A present. Open it." Lisa pulled away the layers of wrapping paper and saw the most gorgeous pyjamas she had ever seen in her life. They were pale sea-green and silky.

She threw her arms round Mum's neck. "They're amazing!" she yelled. "When did you get them?"

"Aha," said Mum. "That's my secret. No more strike, then?"

"No more strike," Lisa agreed, running upstairs with her new pyjamas. She could hardly wait until bedtime to wear them.

In her bedroom, she held the pyjamas up to herself and looked in the mirror. Deciding that she looked beautiful, she was about to go downstairs and thank Mum again when she suddenly noticed that someone was watching her.

In the bedroom opposite, the shadow-dancer's bedroom, she saw Gareth sitting on the bed, looking right at her. And then she realized. Gareth was the shadow-dancer, not his sister! How could she have been so stupid? Boys can be ballet dancers just as much as girls can. She smiled at him, uncertainly. He probably hates me, she thought. He probably thinks I'll tell his friends.

But Gareth was smiling back at her. He opened his bedroom window and signalled for Lisa to do the same. She ran to her window and opened it quickly.

"Do you want to learn how to dance?" he hissed across their two gardens, just loud enough for Lisa to hear, but just quiet enough to make sure that no one else did.

"I'd love to," Lisa hissed back.

"Meet me in your back garden at midnight," Gareth whispered fiercely, and before Lisa had a chance to tell him that midnight was way past her bedtime, he had closed his window and disappeared from view.

That night, when Mum tucked her in and said, "Sleep well", Lisa smiled mysteriously. But the mysterious smile was wasted on Mum, who simply switched off the light and went downstairs.

Lisa felt as if she would burst with excitement. She was going to learn how to dance, and, what's more, her teacher was not going to be just any old person, but Gareth, the expert shadow-dancer.

Luckily it was summer, and easily warm

enough to wear her pyjamas outside. Lisa thought how strange it was that Mum had bought her the new pyjamas just in time for her first dancing lesson. It was almost as if Mum had known somehow.

At five to midnight, Lisa crept downstairs, taking care not to wake Mum, and let herself out through the back door. It was dark outside, but the grass was soft and comforting beneath her feet.

Gareth was already there, waiting for her. He was also wearing pyjamas, red and white stripy ones. Lisa grinned at him.

"Shall we dance?" he said.

# I Don't Like This House!

## Irene Yates

One very sad day Charlotte and her family moved house. "I don't like this house," said Charlotte.

"Nonsense!" said her mother. "It's in a street that's quiet and peaceful."

Charlotte looked out of the window. She looked up the street and down the street. She looked across and beyond, as far as her eyes could see. Where were all the cars and bicycles? Where were all the busy people? Where were all the skipping children?

There were none to be seen. Outside was as quiet as a sleeping lion.

"I don't like this house," said Charlotte.

"Nonsense!" said her mother, "It's got lovely big rooms!"

Charlotte went to explore. She went up the stairs and down the stairs. She went through the doors and round the walls. She peered into the attic and squinted down into the cellar. Where were all the cosy corners? Where were all the crooked walls? Where were all the slanting roofs?

There were none to be seen. All through this house were high, high, ceilings, and walls so long they'd never run out. Inside was vast and echoey as a singing whale.

"I don't like this house," said Charlotte.

"Nonsense!" said her mother. "It's got

lots and lots of cupboard space."

Charlotte opened the cupboards. She opened one under the stairs, but it was empty. She opened two in the kitchen, but there was nothing inside. She opened three in the bedroom, but nothing fell out. Where were all the brooms and buckets? Where were all the pots and pans? Where were the friendly books and the dog-eared teddies?

There were none to be seen. The cupboards were as empty as a hungry bear's cave.

"I don't like this house," said Charlotte.

"Nonsense!" said her mother. "It's got more space."

So Charlotte went back to look at the spaces. She marched through the living room and into the hall. She trotted up the stairs and along the landing. She paced through the bedrooms and shuffled in the bathroom. Where were all the nooks and crannies? Where were all the piled-up corners? Where were all her favourite places?

There were none to be seen. The space was as huge and unfriendly as a biting tiger.

"I don't like this house," said Charlotte.

"Nonsense!" said her mother. "It will be much better for the animals."

So Charlotte went tracking. She looked for Pip's lead, but it wasn't on the hook. She searched for Fluff's basket, but it wasn't by the window. She tried rummaging for Henry's treadwheel, but there was nowhere to rummage. Where were the barks and leaps and licks? Where were the mews and purrs and stretches? Where the squeaks and scrabbles and scratches?

There were none to be found. Everywhere was as still as a sleeping crocodile.

"I don't like this house," said Charlotte.

"Nonsense!" said her mother. "It's got a beautiful back garden. Why don't you go outside and see?"

So Charlotte did. On the slabs where Jamie's pram should be, there was a strawberry tub, with great, fat, juicy strawberries tumbling all over it. Where she expected a rusty old swing to be creaking to and fro, there stood an apple tree, covered with small green apples.

Where she thought she would find a falling-down shed and a heap of dusty bricks, there was a mass of canes spilling with ripe, red tomatoes.

And right in the corner, instead of an overgrown hedge with its prickles and tangles waiting to catch her, there was a forest of bushes oozing with plump raspberries, just begging to be picked. Well!

Charlotte began to pick the raspberries. She collected some early windfall apples from the lawn. She gathered tomatoes for tea. She pulled fat strawberries from the tub and laid them carefully in rows to count. And while she was picking and collecting and gathering and pulling, she

munched and she crunched and she drib-
bled the juice down her chin, and she had
such fun that she didn't hear the removal
van arrive.

Then there was a great humping of
furniture, and an excited scurrying and
sniffing of cats and dogs and hamsters,
and a tremendous welcoming of teddies
and toys and books and pots and pans and
brooms and prams and babies and dads
and everything else. But Charlotte was so
busy with her harvesting that she missed
it all.

At last, when all her fruit was safely
gathered for tea, Charlotte went inside.
Then she looked around in astonishment.
"I like this house," she said happily. "It's
just like home!"

# The Star Money

## Anne Rockwell

There was, once upon a time, a good, kind little girl who had no mother and no father and who was so poor she had no house to live in and no bed to sleep in. She was so poor she had nothing but the clothes she wore and a little piece of bread in her pocket. All alone she went out into the world.

She had not gone far before she met an

old man who said, "Ah, give me something to eat. I am so hungry."

And the little girl gave him her piece of bread and went on again. But before long she met a little child who moaned and said, "My head is cold. Give me something to cover it with."

So she gave him her hat and, when she had walked a little further, she met another child who had no jacket, and he too was cold. So she gave him her own and, a little further on, a child begged for a dress, and she gave that away also. Then she came to a forest, and it was dark.

Soon she met another child who cried and shivered and said, "I am so cold!" And the little girl thought, "It is dark and no one can see me anyway." And so she gave away all the clothes she had.

And as she stood, with not one single thing left, suddenly some stars fell down at her feet. And when she looked, she saw they were not stars at all but shiny gold and silver pieces of money. And although she had just given all her clothes away, she found she was dressed in new ones, much better and warmer than the old. So she put the money in her pocket. Never again was she cold or hungry, and she was happy all the days of her life.

# The Wonderful Washing Machine

## Linda Allen

Mrs Lenska filled up the washing machine with water and when she went to put the clothes in she stared in amazement. "Come here, Henry," she called to Mr Lenska. "Come and see what's happened to the washing machine."

Mr Lenska had a good look. "It seems to be full of strawberry jam," he said at last. "Mm – smells like strawberry jam, too, *tastes* like strawberry jam. It *is* straw-berry jam." He looked sternly at Mrs Lenska. "What have you been doing?" he demanded.

"Nothing," she returned, "except fill it up with water. I don't know how it happened."

"I expect it was those kids from the next apartment," Mr Lenska said. "They're always up to some trick or other."

"It couldn't be them," Mrs Lenska said. "They're away at summer camp. Besides, I haven't opened the door to anyone all morning."

"Well, what are we going to do about it?" asked Mr Lenska. "It's perfectly good jam, but we can't eat that much."

"We'll keep a few pounds of it," Mrs Lenska decided, "and put the rest down the waste disposal. There's nothing else we can do."

So they cleared out the jam and then they cleaned out the washing machine with fresh water, and it was soon working perfectly again. All went well for a few weeks, and then Mrs Lenska noticed something wrong again.

"Henry," she said, "the washing machine's gone peculiar again."

Mr Lenska groaned. "Not more strawberry jam?" he said.

"No," she replied. "This time it seems to be chocolate sauce."

"That's not possible," said Mr Lenska.

"Possible or not," Mrs Lenska retorted, "that's what it is. Taste it and see."

He tasted it, and it was.

"This is ridiculous," he said, "but I'm due in town in an hour's time. I can't stay to help you clean it out this time, but I'll call in and ask the engineer to come and take a look at it."

When the engineer arrived he said it certainly was chocolate sauce, but he didn't seem too surprised. "Would you mind telling me," he asked Mrs Lenska,

"where you bought this machine?"

"I exchanged it for my mahogany table," she told him.

"With Mrs Kalman downstairs?"

"That's right – how did you know?"

"I've been called to this machine before," he replied. "It's had at least five owners to my knowledge. Nobody seems to know what to do with it when it starts behaving like this."

Mrs Lenska was annoyed. "I think Mrs Kalman might have warned me," she said. "After all, my mahogany table doesn't do peculiar things." She glared at the engineer. "Can you fix it?" she asked.

"Well, I'll have a look at it," he said, "but I don't hold out much hope of being able to alter it. Most of the time it works normally, and then something seems to change it altogether." He smiled sadly. "I think it must be magic," he added.

"Magic!" snapped Mrs Lenska scornfully. "There never was any such thing."

"Of course not," murmured the engineer.

He checked all the valves and all the switches; he tried out the motor; he looked at the joints connecting the water to the machine; he even read the instructions on the washing powder packet; but he could find nothing wrong at all.

"That settles it," said Mrs Lenska. "I shall just have to buy a new one. I was saving for something else, but this is more important."

"Are you sure," asked the engineer, "that you can't find a use for this one?"

"Quite sure," she replied. "What on earth could I do with all that strawberry jam and chocolate sauce?"

The engineer shook his head. "What does Mr Lenska think about it?" he enquired.

"Henry thinks exactly as I do," was the answer. "He thinks it's a nuisance and a bad bargain."

"In that case," said the engineer, "I'll tell you what I'll do. I'll ask around. There may be somebody who'd know what to do with it."

"Do that," said Mrs Lenska.

A few weeks later the engineer called again. "Did you buy a new washing machine?" he asked.

"Yes," said Mrs Lenska, "and I haven't had a single problem with it. I can't think why I put up with the other one for so long."

"Have you still got the old one?" asked the engineer.

"Yes," she said. "Have you found some-one to take it off my hands?"

"I think so, if you will take a portable TV for it. Mrs Slinger in the next block is willing to do a deal. She says your old washing machine is exactly what she has been looking for."

Mrs Lenska said, "Henry, go with the man and take a look at Mrs Slinger's portable TV. If it's okay we'll let her have the old washing machine for it."

An hour later the deal was fixed. Mrs Lenska did her washing and watched TV at the same time. She never gave her old washing machine a second thought.

In the next apartment block Mrs Slinger was watching the washing machine with great interest. "I do believe it's vegetable soup!" she cried. "Delicious!" and she and Mr Slinger and the little Slingers had vegetable soup for lunch. When they had finished there was still a lot left. "Go and knock on all the doors in the block," she said, "and tell them there's free soup at the Slingers'. Tell them to bring their own basins."

In no time at all the soup had been gladly received and all that remained to be done was rinse out the washing machine with hot water. After that the machine worked normally for quite a long time, which was a good thing, because Mr and Mrs Slinger had a lot of children and a lot of washing to do, but every once in a while it produced something special – custard, or lemonade, or broth, or ice cream, and always Mrs Slinger shared it out among her neighbours. It never once occurred to her to throw the surplus away.

The engineer called one day. "How are you getting on with the washing machine?" he enquired.

"Fine!" said Mrs Slinger, and explained what was happening and how she was dealing with it.

"I'm glad of that," said the engineer. "I always knew that one day, sooner or later, somebody would know what to do with it."

# The King
# with Dirty Feet

## Pomme Clayton

Once upon a time there was a king. He
lived in a hot, dusty village in India. He
had everything he wanted and was very
happy. But there was one thing that this
king hated and that was bathtime.

Perhaps he was a little bit like you?

This king had not washed for a week,
he had not washed for a month, he had
not washed for a whole year. He had

begun to smell. He smelt underneath his arms, in between his toes, behind his ears and up his nose. He was the smelliest king there has ever been. His servants were all very polite about it, but nobody liked to be in the same room as him. Until one day the smell became too much for even the king himself, and he said rather sadly, "I think it is time I had a bath."

He walked slowly down to the river. The villagers whispered, "The king's going to have a bath!" and they rushed down to the river bank to get the best view.

Everyone fell silent when the king stepped into the cool, clear river water. When he called for the royal soap, a huge cheer arose. He washed himself from top to bottom, scrubbed his hair and brushed his teeth. He played with his little toy ducks and his little boat.

Then, at last, when he was quite clean,

he called for the royal towel and stepped out of the river.

When he had finished drying himself he saw that his feet were covered with dust.

"Oh bother," he cried. "I forgot to wash them." So he stepped back into the water and soaped them well. But as soon as he stood on dry land his feet were dirty again.

"Oh my goodness," he said crossly. "I didn't wash them well enough. Bring me a scrubbing brush." The king scrubbed his feet until they shone. But still, when he stepped on the ground, they were dirty.

This time the king was furious. He shouted for his servant, Gabu. Gabu came running and bowed low before the king.

"Gabu," boomed the king, "the king has had a bath, the king is clean, but the earth is dirty. There is dust everywhere. You must clean the earth so there is no more dust and my feet stay clean."

"Yes, Your Majesty," replied Gabu.

"You have three days in which to rid

the land of dust, and if you fail do you know what will happen to you?" asked the king.

"No, Your Majesty."

"ZUT!" cried the king.

"ZUT?" said Gabu. "What is ZUT?"

"ZUT is the sound of your head being chopped off."

Gabu began to cry.

"Don't waste time, Gabu. Rid the land of dust at once."

The king marched back to his palace.

"I must put my thinking cap on," said Gabu, and he put his head in his hands and began to think.

"When something is dirty, you brush it."

He asked the villagers to help him. They took their brushes and brooms and ONE . . . TWO . . . THREE. . . .

They all began to sweep – swish, swish, swish, swish – all day long.

Until the dust rose up and filled the air in a thick, dark cloud. Everyone was coughing and spluttering and bumping into each other. The king choked, "Gabu, where are you? I asked you to rid the land of dust, not fill the air with dust. Gabu, you have two more days and ZUT!"

"Oh dear, oh dear," cried Gabu, and put his head in his hands and thought.

"When something is dirty, you wash it."

He asked all the villagers to help him. They took their buckets to the well and filled them up to the brims with water and ONE . . . TWO . . . THREE. . . .

They all began to pour – sloosh, sloosh, sloosh, sloosh – all day long.

There was so much water it spread across the land. It began to rise. Soon it was up to their ankles, their knees, their waists and then up to their chests.

"Swim, everybody," cried Gabu.

The king climbed on to the top of the highest mountain where the water lapped his toes and he sniffed, "Gabu, a . . . atchoo! Where are you?"

Gabu came swimming.

"Yes, Your Majesty?"

"Gabu, I asked you to rid the land of dust not turn our village into a swimming pool. You have one more day and ZUT!"

"Oh dear, oh dear, I have run out of ideas," cried Gabu. The water trickled away and Gabu put his head in his hands and thought.

"I could put the king in an iron room with no windows or doors, chinks or cracks, then no speck of dust could creep in. But I don't think he would like that. Oh, if only I could cover up all the dust with a carpet." Then Gabu had a marvellous idea.

"Of course, why didn't I think of this before? Everyone has a needle and thread and a little piece of leather. Leather is tough, we will cover the land with leather."

He asked the villagers to help him. Needles were threaded and knots were tied and ONE . . . TWO . . . THREE. . . .

They all began to sew – stitch, stitch, stitch, stitch – all day long.

Then the huge piece of leather was spread across the land and it fitted perfectly. It stretched from the school to the well, from the temple to the palace, and all the way down to the river.

"We've done it," cried Gabu. "I will go and tell the king."

Gabu knocked on the palace door.

"We are ready, Your Majesty."

The king poked his head carefully around the door not knowing what to expect. Then a little smile twitched at the corners of his mouth. The ground looked clean, very clean indeed. He put one foot on the leather and it was spotless. The king walked across the leather.

"This is splendid, comfortable, clean. Well done, Gabu. Well done."

The king turned to the villagers to thank them.

Suddenly out of the crowd stepped a

little old man with a long white beard and a bent back. Everyone had forgotten him. He bowed low before the king and spoke in a very quiet voice.

"Your Majesty, how will anything be able to grow now that the land is covered with leather? The grass will not be able to push its way through. There will be no vegetables or flowers and no new trees. The animals will be hungry and there will be nothing for us to eat."

Now everyone was listening.

"Your Majesty, you know you don't have to cover the land with leather to keep your feet clean. It is really quite simple."

The old man took out of his pocket a large pair of scissors. He bent down and began to cut the leather very carefully all around the king's feet. Then he took two laces from his pocket and tied each piece of leather to the king's feet. Then he pulled back the leather that covered the earth and said, "Try them, Your Majesty."

The king looked down at his feet covered in leather and frowned. He had never seen anything like it. He put one foot forward.

"Mmm, very good!" he exclaimed. He took another step. "This is splendid, comfortable, clean *and* the grass can grow!"

Then the king walked, then he ran and then he jumped.

"Hooray," he cried. "I can walk here, and here, and here. I can walk anywhere and my feet will always be clean."

What was the king wearing on his feet?

That's right, he was wearing SHOES!

They were the first pair of shoes ever to be made, and people have been wearing them ever since.

# The Brave Cat and the Little Girl

## Margaret Mayo

This is a story told by the Pueblo Indians, and they lived in houses built of bricks made from clay which had been baked in the sun.

Once upon a time, long ago, there was a little Indian girl; and one day her father and mother went out and left her alone in the house with the cat.

At first she liked being in the house all

by herself, but for the cat. She cleaned, and she tidied, and then she began to make a big stew for her supper. And when the cat smelt that stew, he came and brushed gently against her legs. So she gave him some tasty morsels to eat, and he enjoyed that very much. She put the stew in the oven, and then she sat down. And the cat came and sat on her lap; and she stroked his soft, warm fur and did everything she could to make her cat happy.

Then evening came. It grew dark and it was so quiet she could hear the wind whisper outside; and still the girl's father and mother had not returned. Then she was afraid, because she was all alone in the house, but for the cat.

And then her cat spoke.

"Do not be afraid," he said. "Fasten the door and I will take care of you."

So she locked the door and sat down again and waited.

After a while someone came to the door and knocked. The cat jumped down, crept over to the door and peeped through a crack in the wood. And he saw that there was a huge bear, standing outside.

The cat called out: "Please excuse us, Mr Bear, but we are busy building a great big fire and we cannot open the door for you."

The bear waited a little while, and then he knocked again.

"Open the door for me," he said.

But the cat called out: "Please excuse us, Mr Bear, but we are busy making bread and we cannot open the door for you."

The bear waited a little while, and then he knocked for the third time.

"Open the door," he said. "Open the door, for I have presents for you."

"Oh, presents!" said the girl. "I like presents."

But the cat called out: "Please excuse

us, Mr Bear, but the bread is baking in the oven and we cannot open the door for you."

Then the bear began to bang at the door and rattle the lock. He tried his very hardest to break that door down, but it was too strong for him. So at last he began to walk away.

"Open the door," said the cat. And the girl unlocked it and opened it.

Then the cat ran outside and with one long leap, he jumped straight onto the bear's back. And the bear was so frightened that he ran as fast as he could, and as he ran, he dropped a bundle that he held in his arms and out tumbled all sorts of beautiful things. There was a lovely dress, beaded slippers and a whole heap of fine bracelets and necklaces.

When the girl saw this, she hurried out and gathered up the beautiful things. Then she took them into the house and dressed herself in the new dress and the beaded slippers and all the fine bracelets and necklaces. And then the cat came back.

Presently the girl's father and mother came home, and they *were* surprised to see their daughter dressed in such beautiful clothes. And when she told them how she had got them from a bear, they could not understand it. But they were so pleased to see that she was safe and well that they said no more about it.

The weeks passed by, and then one day the father and mother went out again and left the girl alone in the house with the cat. And she was glad to stay at home, for she hoped the bear would come once more and bring her presents.

Again she cleaned and tidied the house and made a big stew for her supper. But when the cat came sidling up to her and brushed against her legs as if to say, "I'd like some of that," she pushed him away.

She said, "You do not give me presents

103

like the bear. You shall not have any of my stew."

So the cat climbed up onto a shelf and pretended to go to sleep.

Then it grew dark and very quiet, and the girl began to be afraid.

But the cat said, "Do not be afraid. Fasten the door and I will take care of you."

"I will not fasten the door," said the girl, "for maybe the bear will come and bring me presents."

So the cat closed his eyes and pretended to go to sleep again.

That night the bear did come. He knocked at the door, opened it, and walked right in.

The girl was so pleased to see the bear, even though it was plain that he had not a bundle in his arms.

"Good evening, Mr Bear," she said. "Do come and sit down."

And the bear came and sat down beside

her, and he looked at her very hard. So then the girl looked back at the bear.

"Mr Bear," she said, "tell me, why are your feet so big?"

"To walk the faster, little girl. To walk the faster."

"And why is your nose so long?"

"To smell the keener, little girl. To smell the keener."

"And why are your ears so big?"

"To hear the sharper, little girl. To hear the sharper."

"And why are your eyes so bright?"

"To see the farther, little girl. To see the farther."

"And why are your teeth so long?"

"TO EAT YOU UP!"

With that he grabbed hold of the girl and lifted her up and ran out of the house. And he ran and he ran and *he ran* towards his den.

Then the cat jumped off the shelf, and he ran right after that bear, and with one long leap, he jumped straight onto the bear's head. And he scratched him and scratched him and *scratched him*, until the bear dropped the girl and threw himself on the ground and cried for mercy.

Then the cat took the girl back to her own house.

And when her father and mother came home, she was sitting by the fire, quite safe and sound, with the cat on her lap, and she was stroking him.

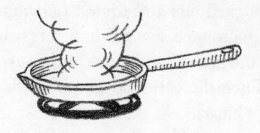

# The Story of the Thick Fat Pancake

## Traditional

There once was a mother who had seven hungry children. She took flour, milk, butter, eggs, sugar – not forgetting just a pinch of salt – and made a beautiful thick fat pancake. It lay in the pan, and it swelled up until it was a joy to see. The seven children stood round about, and the grandfather looked over the mother's shoulder.

"Mother, dear Mother, please give me the pancake," said the first child.

"Dear, kind Mother," said the second, "please give it to me."

"Dear, kind, beautiful Mother," said the third, "please give it to me."

"Dear, kind, beautiful, good Mother," said the fourth, "please give it to me."

"Dear, kind, beautiful, good, sweet Mother," said the fifth, "please give it to me."

"Dear, kind, beautiful, good, sweet, wonderful Mother," said the sixth, "please give it to me."

"Dear, kind, beautiful, good, sweet, wonderful, marvellous Mother," said the seventh, "please give it to me."

But Mother replied, "Wait till it is turned."

Hardly had the words left her mouth than the pancake began to think, "I should turn over, should I? But I am far too beautiful to be eaten. I think I shall go out into the wide world and seek my fortune!"

So it leapt out of the pan and scuttled across the floor, hoppity-hop, and out of the door.

"Come back!" cried Mother as she ran after it, still clutching the pan and ladle, while Grandfather and all the seven children followed behind her.

They all shouted, "Come back, come back!" But the pancake bounced hoppity-hop downstairs and out into the street.

There it met a cat, and when the cat saw the fine thick fat pancake, she said, "Miaow, miaow, thick fat pancake, please let *me* eat you!"

But the pancake said, "What! Shall I be eaten by you, little cat? Mother couldn't catch me, Grandfather couldn't catch me, seven squalling children couldn't catch me. Do you think I can't escape you too?"

And it ran, hoppity, hoppity, hoppity, along the street.

By and by along came a cock, who said, "Dear thick fat pancake, please let *me* eat you!"

"What!" said the pancake. "Shall I be eaten by you, little cock? Mother couldn't catch me, Grandfather couldn't catch me, seven squalling children and the cat couldn't catch me. Do you think I can't escape you too?"

And it ran, hoppity, hoppity, hoppity, on into the wide world.

By and by it met a goose, who said, "Clackety, clackety clack, fat pancake, let *me* eat you!"

"What!" said the pancake. "Shall I be eaten by you, little goose? Mother couldn't catch me, Grandfather couldn't catch me, seven squalling children and the cat and the cock couldn't catch me. Do you think I can't escape you too?"

And it ran, hoppity, hoppity, faster than ever into the wide world.

By and by along came a cow, who said,

"Moo, moo, thick fat pancake, let *me* eat you!"

"What!" said the pancake once again. "Shall I be eaten by you, little cow? Mother couldn't catch me, Grandfather couldn't catch me, seven squalling children and the cat and the cock and the goose couldn't catch me. Do you think I can't escape you too?"

And it ran, hoppity, hoppity, hoppity, faster than ever into the wide world.

Along came two little children, a boy and a girl. They were very hungry because they had had nothing to eat all day long. When they saw the thick fat pancake they cried, "Pancake, dear pancake, do let *us* eat you!"

But the pancake replied: "What! Shall I be eaten by you, little Johnny-Jenny? Mother couldn't catch me, Grandfather couldn't catch me, seven squalling children and the cat and the cock and the goose and the cow couldn't catch me. Do you think I can't escape you too?"

And it ran, hoppity, hoppity, hoppity, faster than ever into the wide world.

Along came a pig, who said, "Come here, thick fat pancake, and let *me* eat you!"

"What!" said the pancake once again. "Shall I be eaten by you, little pig? Mother couldn't catch me, Grandfather couldn't catch me, seven squalling children and the cat and the cock and the goose and the cow and little Johnny-Jenny couldn't catch me. Do you think I can't escape you too?"

And it ran, hoppity, hoppity, hoppity, faster than ever into the wide world.

But then the pancake came to a brook, and it did not know how to cross over to the other side, for there was no bridge. It ran hoppity, hoppity along the bank, looking for a way to get across.

Now the pig threw itself into the water and swam downstream after the pancake.

But the pancake was afraid of getting wet, so the pig said, "Would you like me to carry you across, thick fat pancake?"

"Yes, please," said the pancake.

"Then jump on to my back, or better still, on to my snout," said the pig.

So the pancake leapt on to the pig's snout, but hardly had it landed there when snap! the pig bit it in half, and swallowed one half without delay; but the other half leapt on to the other bank, and scuttled away, hoppity, hop. The pig grunted, and snuffled along after it, but never caught it.

And that is why pigs always snuffle with their snout on the ground, because they are all still hoping to find the other half of the thick fat pancake.

# Jasper the
# Vain Toucan
## Angela McAllister

Jasper was a vain toucan who plumed and preened and peered at his reflection all day long.

He was especially proud of his beautiful beak which he polished with great care and displayed for all the creatures of the jungle to admire as he swaggered splendidly by.

All the creatures of the jungle thought

Jasper was quite silly.

"A beak is for catching food," they said disapprovingly.

But Jasper was so proud of his beak that he wouldn't use it to catch food in case it got scratched and dirty.

So the other toucans shared their food with Jasper.

"He may be quite silly, but we birds of a feather must stick together," they agreed. "One day Jasper will change . . ."

But Jasper only changed for the worse!

He became more and more boastful of his handsome beak. Every day he posed grandly on a rock in the middle of the river to be more easily admired from all sides.

One afternoon as he gazed at his reflection in the water Jasper had an outrageous idea. "If I had a beak of GOLD I would dazzle everybody with my brilliance!" he thought excitedly. "Then nobody could deny I was the most magnificent bird in the whole jungle!"

But where was he to find a beak of gold?

Jasper remembered something he had heard about a Miracle Bird who lived deep in the heart of the jungle. The Miracle Bird was as old as the ancient rivers and could do strange and wonderful things.

"Maybe he could give me a beak of gold," thought Jasper.

So he set off into the heart of the jungle to find the Miracle Bird.

As he searched the deep darkness Jasper came to a clearing lit by a single shaft of light. And there on a knot of tangled roots sat the Miracle Bird.

Jasper had expected to find a fabulous creature with bright feathers and a magnificent tail. But instead he was surprised to see a small black bird with one curled tail feather and sleepy green eyes. Jasper introduced himself and explained that he was looking for a gold beak.

The Miracle Bird blinked dreamily.

"Are you *sure* you want a gold beak?" he asked.

"Oh yes, more than anything, I do want a gold beak," answered Jasper eagerly.

"More than *anything*?" said the Miracle Bird, peering at the toucan closely.

Jasper could not think of anything better than being the most handsome creature in the jungle. "More than ANYTHING!" he insisted.

"Well, I think you are being quite silly," said the Miracle Bird, "but if that is what you really want you must eat the fruit of this ancient Orinoco tree and drink the water where the sunlight falls."

Jasper was too excited about his beak to consider whether he was being quite silly. He ate the fruit and drank from the sunlit water and waited impatiently for something to happen.

"Don't just stand there like a toucan," said the Miracle Bird wearily.

"But I am a toucan!" replied Jasper, staring hard at his beak.

"You may return home. And by the time you arrive you will have a beak of pure gold," promised the Miracle Bird, and with a deep sigh he shut his eyes and went to sleep.

Jasper set off home, full of expectation. And, as he flew among the giant trees of the jungle, his beak caught the light and shone brighter and brighter.

But as it grew golden it also grew heavy, and soon Jasper was too heavy to fly.

So he continued his journey on foot. But the beautiful gold beak weighed heavier and heavier until he could hardly lift his head from the ground. Finally, as he came to a slimy swamp, Jasper's gold beak glinted brilliantly and then sank deep into the mud. And no matter how hard he tugged, he could not pull himself free. Jasper felt quite silly standing on tiptoes with his beak in the mud, looking at the world upside down. "I do hope nobody comes along and sees me like this," he thought.

But as the day passed, Jasper started to feel bored and lonely. He tried tugging again but the gold beak was firmly stuck in the mud and too heavy to pull out.

Jasper wished he was back on the rock in the middle of the river with his old polished beak in all its glory . . .

The day passed and the night came and poor Jasper had to sleep on his tiptoes, upside down.

In the morning he was hungry but there was nobody to pull him out and feed him. Soon he started to look thin and ragged and muddy.

"I wish I didn't have this heavy gold beak," sighed Jasper to himself, "I wish I had my old beak back. More than anything I wish I had an ordinary toucan's beak . . ."

"More than *anything*?" said a small voice from the undergrowth.

Poor Jasper couldn't look up but he heard a rustle of leaves and there before him he saw the tiny black feet of the Miracle Bird.

Jasper couldn't think of anything better than being an ordinary toucan with a beak light enough for flying and perfect for catching food – no matter *what* it looked like.

"More than ANYTHING!" he said in his muffled voice.

"Well, let that be an end to all this nonsense," said the Miracle Bird kindly.

And with a jerk Jasper fell back out of the swamp, pulling his old beak out of the mud.

"I have been quite silly, haven't I?" said Jasper shyly, as he accustomed himself to being downside up again.

"You *were* quite silly but now you have changed," the Miracle Bird assured him. And with a wink of his bright eye he hopped back to the heart of the jungle.

At last Jasper flew home light and free. When the other toucans saw him they hardly recognized the thin, ragged, muddy bird before them.

But Jasper would not tell anyone about his quite silly adventure. "I shan't be going on any more journeys," he told them. "I've had enough change for one toucan. And after all, we ordinary birds of a feather must stick together."

And he flew off to gather food for them all to share . . .

# The Toffee Join

## William Mayne

"It's raining," said Diana. She huffed her breath on to the window and drew on the steamy mark with her finger. She drew a smile and a nose and two eyes, but before she could draw the chin and the hair and the ears the mark had gone away.

"It's been raining all day," said Mother. "That's why I'm sitting quietly at home doing some darning. That's why your brother wants to go out and play in the garden. He always goes by contraries."

"Granny said," said Diana, "that next time it was raining and we hadn't anything to do, she would like me to take her half a pound of treacle."

"Yes," said Mother, "that would be a good idea. But before you do that you'd better go to Michael's house, and then to Mervyn and Susan's house, and see whether they have to take anything on the next wet day when they've got nothing to do."

"Why would they want to go there?" said Diana.

"Why," said Mother, "she's Granny to all of you, isn't she? You put your coat on and ask Michael whether he wants to go, and then ask the other two as well."

Diana came down from the window. "I shall forget what I've gone for," she said. "They're all bigger than me. Can't we send Robin? Isn't that what brothers are for?"

But Mother thought that Diana could manage; and she helped her on with her coat, and opened the door, and pulled up her hood, and sent her off. "I shall watch you," said Mother. "I can see your red coat from a long way off."

Diana went down the path, out of the gate, and along the side of the road close to the wall. In the village where she lived there was no pavement, so everybody had to walk in the road.

Michael's house was nearly next door, and Michael was lying by the fire scuffing the carpet up with his boots.

"What do *you* want?" he said. He did not think Diana was the sort of visitor you have to be polite to. Diana explained that it was a wet day and there was nothing to do, and that Granny wanted half a pound of treacle.

"What about it, then?" said Michael.

"We're going to take her some," said Diana. "Me and Robin. Mother thought you might want to go."

"No. I'm all right here," said Michael. But his mother, who was sister to Diana's mother, came through from her kitchen and said: "Yes, you do want to go to Granny's, because she said that next time it rained and I couldn't keep you from scuffing up the carpet with your boots, you had to go up there and take her four ounces of butter. So I'll just get that ready, and then you can be off with Diana and her treacle."

Michael got up from the fireside. "Oh well," he said. "If they all want looking after, then I suppose I'd better go." And he let his face go into a way that meant he did a lot for other people and never got thanked; but putting his face like that made his chin tickle itself, and he ended up by laughing.

Diana said she would go and get the

other two, the other cousins with the same granny, Mervyn and Susan.

Mervyn and Susan had something to do already. They were putting together a big jigsaw puzzle. All they had was the edge, so that it looked like a picture that had been rubbed out; though it was really a picture that had not been rubbed in yet.

"Can I lay some?" said Diana; and she put in a piece that seemed to fit, and she wondered why Mervyn or Susan had not done it before.

"That's wrong," said Susan. "I'm sorry to say, my dear girl." That was the way she sometimes talked. She got it from going to school and being in the middle class. All the other cousins were in the bottom class, except Diana, and she was in no class at all.

Mervyn and Susan's mother asked Diana why she had come out on such a wet day. Diana told her that they could all go to Granny's, because Granny wanted some treacle and some butter.

"Oh yes," said Susan. "And one day she wants half a pound of sugar, she said."

"I remember," said Susan's mother. "And I think today would be a good day for you to take it." So they weighed out half a pound of sugar and poured it into a bag, and turned the top of the bag over like the end of a sleeve that is too long. Mervyn put on his duffel coat with the wooden pegs instead of buttons, and put the sugar in his pocket. Susan put on her orange raincoat, and her mother blinked at her and Diana, because one of them was red and the other one was orange.

"You do clash," she said.

Michael was ready at his house. The butter was in a piece of greaseproof paper, in his anorak pocket. It had to be pushed back in now and then in case it fell out. "I wasn't bringing any basket," he said. "I don't want to be messing on with baskets."

They went to Diana's house, and stood in a row in the kitchen.

"What a lot of us," said Mother, putting them all in order of height and age. Tallest was Susan, then Michael, then Mervyn, then Robin, and then Diana. Robin was the fat one.

"Just what to put the treacle in," said Mother. "I know, I'll put it in a plastic bag, and that'll be easy to carry, and hard to break, and the rain won't get into it. If some clever fingers will hold the bag open I'll pour the treacle in."

There were five clever fingers, one from each person, so that the bag was held very wide open while Mother spooned in half a jar of golden syrup. It sat all smiling in the clear plastic. Robin, of course, let go of his piece of the bag when he wriggled his holding finger straight and got a nailful of treacle. He licked it off when the job was done. Mother twisted the neck of the bag round on itself and tied a knot, and

131

gave the bag to Diana to carry. She said that Robin would be untwisting it and getting his fingers in.

"*I* won't," said Diana. "I'm good." She was good until Mother knelt down in front of her to pull her socks to her knees for her. Then Diana sat the golden bagful on the back of Mother's neck.

"Oh, it does feel funny," said Mother, rubbing the back of her neck to see whether any treacle had got out on to it. None had. All the others had to have the cold clingy bag on the backs of their necks too. Then Mother said they were ready to go, and sent them out of the door and down the garden and over the stile into the field. In the field there was a path made of big flat flagstones, and they walked along it in a line, with Diana in front, and Susan at the back.

"We look after the boys," said Diana. "We're mothers."

"I'd rather have the cat," said Michael,

but the other two did not mind at all.

The path led them across the field and to another wall with a stile in it. It was a high wall, and there were some steps up to it, and down the other side. Here they met a dog they knew called Rover. He was waiting for his master, who was working in a barn close by. Rover stood in the middle of the stile, and he would not get out of the way for Diana.

"Out of the way, good boy," said Diana, pushing at him with one hand. In the other hand was the bag of treacle. But Rover stood at the top of the steps and looked down at her, and wagged his tail slowly, and looked right over Diana's head at the far distance.

Robin came next, with his hands tight in his pockets so that he looked fatter than ever. Rover looked at him, and gave him a nudge with his nose, so that Robin fell down in the rain off the steps, and rolled in the grass. He got up still smiling, because he nearly always smiled, and waited to see how the other two boys managed. Mervyn was next, and he had a pull at Rover's collar, but Rover hunched his shoulders and would not come. Then Michael tried to push Rover, and Rover seemed to think Michael was stronger, and he went backwards down the steps the other side of the stile. It was hard work for Michael, because he had to put one arm round Rover's neck and heave and heave. But at last Rover was out of the way, and they all went through the stile. Rover sat down in the lane, and began to undo some paper he had found, and lick what was inside.

Michael found what it was when he looked in his pocket. Rover had taken the butter from the pocket, and that was what he had unwrapped. When Michael ran back to him, Rover had finished the butter and left the paper. He gave Michael a buttery kiss on the cheek, and went back to watching the stile.

"Never mind," said Susan. "It'll give him a bad pain, and then he'll be sorry; and we'll tell Granny, and she won't mind if you haven't brought any butter."

"We can have jam and bread without butter," said Diana.

Michael picked up the empty paper, and put that in his pocket, just to show Granny when they got there. Then they all ran down the lane. They were careful to run in the middle of it, because it was a muddy lane where tractors came, and along both sides there were muddy ruts full of water. Along the middle there was grass.

Then they ran on to a hard flat piece of lane, where somebody had made the ground firm with stones.

They were slippery stones. First Mervyn skidded and rolled over, and then Robin, who rolled much further. Then Diana was next. She skidded on the stones and sat down.

Michael and Susan stopped running before they came to the slippery part. Susan came to help Diana get up.

"Did you hurt yourself?" said Susan.

"No," said Diana. "Isn't it funny, it was quite soft."

"Good," said Susan. She went to pick the boys up, and left Diana to get up on her own. They all got up, and found that no one was hurt; and they ran on again. Granny's house was beyond the end of the lane, through another field, and they were nearly there.

Diana found she was not carrying the treacle any more. She had dropped it. She thought it was a good thing it had not been in a glass jar, or in a tin the lid could fall from. She looked round, and found the bag, sitting on the stony ground like a blister. She picked it up and ran on with the others.

She went past Susan and Michael and Robin, and she was just going to run past

Mervyn when Susan called to her to stop, because the treacle was getting out.

Diana stopped, and looked at the treacle. One of the corners of the bag had split, and the golden stuff was running slowly out and leaving a trail on the grass of the lane.

"Stop it running out," said Susan. But they did not know how to stop it running. Diana put her finger against it, but the treacle ran round her finger, and she had to suck it dry. Mervyn thought a leaf might do it, if he pressed it on firmly. But the leaf fell off with the treacle. Michael thought Diana should hold the bag upside down, but that was too difficult to do.

"Then we'll just hurry," said Susan. "And get there before it all runs out. Quick, run."

So they ran again, through the gate at the end of the lane, and across the field, where there was only a track, and through another gate into the rest of the lane, and there was Granny's house.

They all ran up to the door, and they all banged on it. Even Robin banged with his head. He had taken one hand from his pocket, but he was using that to catch the trailing treacle, a fingerful at a time.

Granny came to the door, and there was such a noise when she did, because everybody spoke at once. She had to tell them all to be quiet, and then make Susan say what they all wanted.

"A plate," said Susan, "please, Granny, very quickly."

Granny brought a plate very quickly, and Diana lifted up the treacle bag and laid it on the plate. But they were too late. The treacle had finished running out. Instead of a full, fat, golden bag there was a thin, wrinkled, empty one, with a few drops of gold here and there. And that was all.

"Oh dear," said Granny. "It does look

out of breath, doesn't it? What happened?"

Susan explained how nearly all of them had fallen down, and the treacle bag had fallen too. Then she told Granny how they had met Rover, and Rover had eaten the butter he had taken from Michael's pocket.

"But is the sugar safe?" said Granny. "That will be something."

"Of course it is," said Mervyn, patting his pocket. He put his hand in, and pulled out the paper bag and held it up to Granny. But all the sugar stayed in his pocket, because the bottom had come out of the bag.

He took off his coat, and Granny tipped his pocket out. There was half a pound of sugar, a toffee paper, a piece of chewing-gum, a length of string, two hazelnuts, a tooth from his own mouth, and a tooth he had picked up in a field, an apple core not quite eaten down to the middle yet, a bendy potato crisp, and two stones tied together with wire, part of an invention. There was a lot of grimy dust as well. And the sugar had turned damp, and turned grey too.

"Well," said Granny, "you haven't brought me any of the things I asked for, have you? But you needn't be sad about it, because it was no one's fault, was it?"

"It was naughty Rover, and the slippery stones, and just the oldness of the bag," said Susan. "They couldn't help that, could they, all these little ones?"

"No, they couldn't," said Granny. "And we old ones, that's you and me, Susan, will get some more sugar and treacle and butter from the cupboard and start from the beginning. And all the little ones can take off their wet things and hang them up to dry. And you'll all have to sit on the floor to take your boots and shoes off."

It was a stone floor, but there were sacks on it, because the day was so wet, to stop wet footprints. They all sat on the sacks and took off their shoes and boots. Diana sat on one with a red diamond on it, and took off her shoes. She undid the laces. Robin pulled off his boots. He had to use both his fat little hands.

When Diana stood up, the sack stood up with her. It had stuck to the back of her knees. Granny said: "What are you doing, bairn?"

"The floor has got up with me," said Diana. Granny came and pulled the sack away.

"No wonder," said Granny. "You know where all that treacle went? It's all over the back of your knees. How did you manage that?"

"I know," said Susan. "She said the ground wasn't very hard when she slipped and sat down. She must have sat on the treacle bag, and that's what burst it."

So Granny stopped weighing half a pound of sugar, and stood Diana in the sink instead, with her socks on, and washed the socks and the treacle off together. Then she dried Diana's legs very briskly, and hung the wet socks by the stove to dry by themselves. Diana wished she were a sock, because it seemed to have an easier life.

"Now we can get on with the Toffee Join," said Granny, drying her hands and beginning to pour treacle from a tin on to the weighed sugar. "A Toffee Join is when people bring things to have them made into toffee, and when they've made the toffee they eat it," she said. "You all brought things, and I was going to make it with my pan and my stove. But now we'll make it with all my things, and share it out in the old-fashioned way, the same as my grandmother used to when I was a girl."

The butter went into the pan first, and cracked itself smooth and hot. Then the sugar and the syrup went in on top of that, and the pan went quiet again.

Granny stirred and stirred with a wooden spoon. She said that no one must come too near, because toffee was hotter than the hottest water in the hottest kettle. She sent Susan to get a saucer of water, and stood that on the table. Robin wanted to know why it wasn't a saucer of milk. Granny said it was so that she could see to the bottom of the saucer, and no one could see through milk. The cat jumped on the table and looked into the saucer, and thought it was empty, and went down again.

"Not for you, puss," said Granny. It was for testing the toffee. The toffee had begun to bubble in the pan, and a quick steam was coming from it. Granny picked some of the hot melted toffee up in the spoon and poured it into the water. They all looked into the saucer. The toffee squirmed, and then stood still. Granny picked it up in her fingers. It was warm, she said. Then she squeezed it, and then she ate it. "My first taste," she said. "Not quite ready yet."

The next time she tried it, it was ready. She told all five of them to stand by the table, while she walked across the kitchen with the pan. She told them to look out of the window and not watch her, because what happened next was the surprise part of a Toffee Join.

At the end of her kitchen was a very big stone slab, like a table with one edge built into the wall. Usually it was covered with things like bread bins and crockery. Today it was empty, and that was where Granny went.

They could hear her pouring and scraping, and then they heard her put the pan down. Robin kept trying to turn himself round to have a look, and Diana kept turning him back.

"Don't look yet," said Granny, and they heard her doing something with a knife. Then, when she had finished that she

sent them all through into her sitting-room. There was no toffee there, but tea was all ready by the fire. So they had tea. Then, when they had finished tea Granny went into the kitchen again, saying that the Toffee Join was nearly ready. And then she called them through.

Now there was a white cloth spread on the big stone, with one edge folded back very neatly like a bed. And like little people asleep in the bed were five ends of toffee bars, lying on the stone, because at a Toffee Join the toffee is always spread on a stone slab in strips, with just the ends left showing, and each person chooses a piece, so that some get long pieces and some get short ones. No one can tell what is under the cloth and out of sight.

"Youngest first, this time," said Granny. "Diana."

"This one," said Diana, pointing.

"Put your finger on it," said Granny. And when each person came up to

146

choose, they were told to put a finger on what they had chosen. When they had finished, Granny turned the cloth back. They saw that Robin had the longest piece, and Diana a middle-sized piece, and poor Susan had the shortest piece of all. Some people looked pleased, like Robin, and some looked sad, like Susan.

"I knew it would be like that," said Granny, and she pulled the cloth right back, and there was another piece for each person, arranged so that the person with the longest piece now would get a short one later, and the person with the shortest piece now would get the longest later. So that everybody was pleased.

"Well, look at that," said Granny, when she had got a knife and was going to lift the toffee from its place. They all looked, and they saw that the naughty cat had walked right across the toffee and left its footprints on every bar.

"It didn't touch the toffee," said

Granny. "It walked across the cloth I put on top. Look, there are its footprints."

There were ten bars of toffee, and there was a big puddle of it next to the bars, where Granny had poured all the rest. It was the biggest share, she said. Then she said, "What a funny shape it has on its top. Why, I do believe that bad cat has walked across all the toffee bars and curled up on the biggest piece of all and gone to sleep."

"You can see where its elbows were," said Susan.

"It would be nice and warm to lie on," said Granny. "And soft as well. It's a good thing there was a cloth on it, or the cat would have stuck down worse than Diana did. And cats are very bad to wash. They don't like it."

"I know what you can do, Granny," said Susan. "You can cut up the cat shape, and it can be a sort of toffee jigsaw puzzle, pussy-cat shape."

So Granny cut it up, and they muddled it up, and put it together, and then put it in three little paper bags, and took it home to eat the next day.

"And on another wet day," said Granny, "we'll have another Toffee Join."

## Acknowledgements

Every effort has been made by the publishers to trace the owners of the copyright in the stories in this book. If any are inadvertently wrongly attributed, they will be happy to correct this in the event of a reprint. They are grateful to the following copyright holders for permission to use their stories:

Scholastic Publications Ltd for *The Flood* by Ruth Ainsworth from *Ten Tales of Shellover*; and *I Don't Like This House* by Irene Yates from *Stories to Read Aloud* compiled by Ian Souter; Laura Cecil Literary Agency for *Helping Lizzie Sleep* by Adèle Geras and *Simple Jack* retold by James Reeves; Professor Riordan for *Mashenka and the Bear* by James Riordan; Pomme Clayton for *The King with Dirty Feet* by Pomme Clayton; The Jane Gregory Agency for *Pyjama Dance* by Sophie Hannah; Curtis Brown New York for *The Star Money* from *The Three Bears and Other Stories* by Anne Rockwell; Rogers, Coleridge and White for *The Wonderful Washing Machine* by Linda Allen; Reed Consumer Books Ltd for *The Brave Cat and the Little Girl* from *The Book of Magical Cats* by Margaret Mayo; The Bodley Head for *The Story of the Thick Fat Pancake* from *My Big First Story Book* by Richard Bamberger; David Higham Associates for *The Toffee Join* by William Mayne.

### Josie Smith by Magdalen Nabb

Josie Smith lives with her mum in an industrial town; she is a resourceful, independent little girl who always does what she thinks best, but often lands herself in trouble.

### Josie Smith at the Seaside by Magdalen Nabb

Josie Smith makes friends with a girl called Rosie Margaret; with the donkey, Susie; and with a big friendly dog called Jimmie, who swims off with Josie Smith's new bucket.

### Josie Smith at School by Magdalen Nabb

More muddles and misunderstandings for Josie Smith. She is horribly late for lessons when she tries to get a present for her new teacher. And then she helps her new friend to write a story and completely forgets to do her own homework!

### Josie Smith and Eileen by Magdalen Nabb

Josie Smith doesn't always like Eileen because Eileen has things that Josie Smith longs for – a birthday party, a bride doll, and the chance to be a bridesmaid in a long shiny pink frock. But Josie is happy in the end.

You can see Josie Smith in the Granada TV serial, *Josie Smith*.

**All at £3.50**

# JOSIE SMITH
## by Magdalen Nabb

Collect all the colours of the rainbow with Josie Smith's seven rainbow-coloured books!

Josie lives with her mum. She is resourceful and independent and always does what she thinks best, which often lands her in trouble.

Josie Smith
Josie Smith at the Seaside
Josie Smith at School
Josie Smith and Eileen
Josie Smith at Christmas
Josie Smith in Hospital
Josie Smith at the Market

£2.99

# THE ENCHANTED HORSE
## by Magdalen Nabb

The magical story of Irina, a little girl who finds a dusty wooden horse in a junk shop. Irina's mother and father have little time for her, even though it is Christmas, so Irina spends all her time loving and caring for the little horse made of wood – until one night, the horse stamps its hooves and whisks Irina away on an enchanted gallop through the night. This is the first of many secret rides, but when the enchanted horse hears the hooves of the wild horses, she gallops away from Irina who fears she'll never see her beloved horse again. But she does come back, and leaves Irina a very special present.

£2.99

# Monty the Dog Who Wears Glasses

# Monty Bites Back

# Monty Must be Magic

# Monty – Up to his Neck in Trouble

# Monty Ahoy!
### by Colin West

Monty's glasses are supposed to remind him to look where he's going, but they don't seem to work very well. He has a habit of landing in trouble, whether it's chasing the cat next door, falling in the custard or pinching sausages. But whatever happens, Monty, the dog who wears glasses, always manages to come out on top!

£2.99

# MORE STORIES
# FOR SIX-YEAR-OLDS

Have you heard the story of the woman who lived in a vinegar bottle? Or seen the wild little house which went for a walk to the seaside? Read about the fat grandmother, little Jenny Miller and Betsey with her magic marble!

More entertaining stories by Margaret Mahy, Malorie Blackman, Eleanor Farjeon and others, specially chosen for readers of around six years old, by children's book expert Julia Eccleshare.

£3.50

# Order Form

To order direct from the publishers, just make a list of the titles you want and fill in the form below:

Name ................................................................................

Address ...........................................................................

.........................................................................................

.........................................................................................

Send to:  Dept 6, HarperCollins Publishers Ltd, Westerhill Road, Bishopbriggs, Glasgow G64 2QT.

Please enclose a cheque or postal order to the value of the cover price, plus:

**UK & BFPO**: Add £1.00 for the first book, and 25p per copy for each addition book ordered.

**Overseas and Eire**: Add £2.95 service charge.  Books will be sent by surface mail but quotes for airmail despatch will be given on request.

A 24-hour telephone ordering service is avail-able to Visa and Access card holders: 041-772 2281